31472400281923

TWO SPECKLED EGGS

Jennifer K. Mann

CANDLEWICK PRESS

GINGER'S BIRTHDAY PARTY was in two weeks, and she wanted to invite all the girls in her class . . .

except Lyla Browning.

Lyla Browning was weird: she smelled like old leaves,
she didn't talk much, and she even brought a tarantula
in a pickle jar for Show-and-Tell.

It's a curly-
hair tarantula!

But Ginger's mom said she had to invite all of the girls in her class—or none of them.

Since "none of them" wouldn't be a very fun birthday party, Ginger invited all of them— even Lyla Browning.

When the doorbell rang on the day of the party, Ginger ran to answer it.

It was Lyla Browning. She was very early.

Finally, the doorbell rang again—and then
again and again and again.

The girls piled their presents on the table,
then ran off to play the party games.

But Ava changed all the rules to Blindman's Bluff.

And Caroline dropped the egg for the egg-and-spoon race before it even started.

Then Maya and Julia stuck all the tails for Pin the Tail on the Donkey on each other.

"You're wrecking all the games!" yelled Ginger.
But the girls had already started the three-legged race.

Finally it was time for silver-and-gold cake, Ginger's favorite. But Maggie didn't like coconut and Sara wouldn't eat the pineapple part. The rest of the girls just picked at the frosting and didn't touch the cake.

Except Lyla Browning.

Maybe "none of them" would have been a better party after all, Ginger thought as the girls ran off, giggling. She scrunched up her eyes, but the tears fell out anyway.

Just then something landed on Ginger's nose—a ladybug!
Ginger crossed her eyes to look at it.

Lyla Browning laughed. So did Ginger.

At last it was time for presents.
Ginger opened them one by one.

Lyla Browning's was the last present.

Ginger opened the flaps of the brown box and
pulled out what looked like a tiny bird's nest.

Lyla had made it herself, she said, out of paper, tinsel, ribbon, and string. In the center were two speckled eggs.

"They're chocolate—malted milk!" Lyla whispered.

"Oh!" gasped Ginger. "I love malted-milk eggs!"

"Me too," said Lyla.

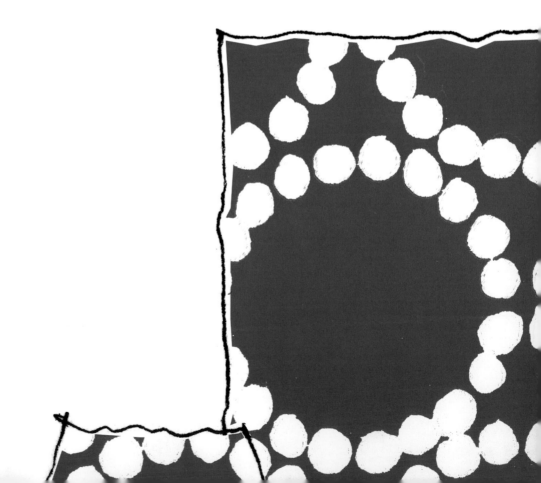

Later, when everyone else was gone, Ginger gave Lyla one of the eggs.

Then Ginger and Lyla pretended they were birds and pecked at the rest of the birthday cake until Lyla had to go home.

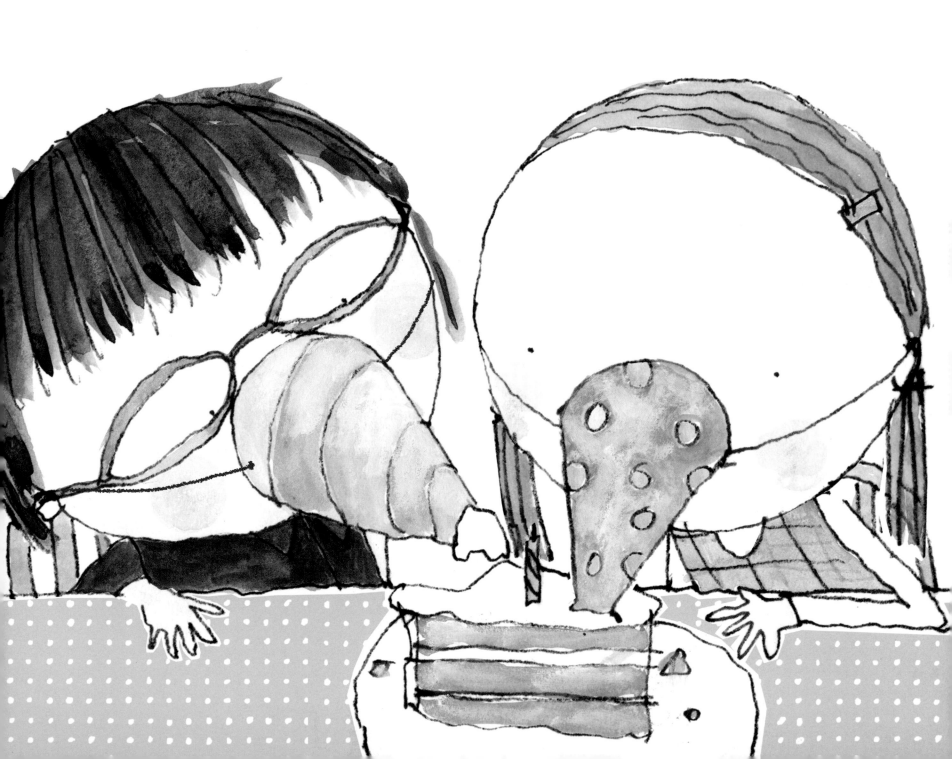

No one else carried a magnifying glass in her pocket or made bird's nests for birthday presents.

And no one else knew that silver-and-gold cake and two speckled eggs could make a birthday perfect.

Except Lyla Browning . . . and Ginger.

For S. D. G.,
cake maker, memory keeper, cheerleader, mom.
Wish you were here to see this.

First edition 2014

Library of Congress Catalog Card Number 2013944009
ISBN 978-0-7636-6168-7

14 15 16 17 18 19 TLF 10 9 8 7 6 5 4 3 2 1

Printed in Dongguan, Guangdong, China

This book was typeset in Caecilia.
The illustrations were done in pencil, gouache,
and digital collage.

Candlewick Press
99 Dover Street
Somerville, Massachusetts 02144

visit us at www.candlewick.com